Toot & Puddle

Get With the Beat

Based on the teleplay by James R. Backshall
Adapted by Laura F. Marsh

NATIONAL GEOGRAPHIC
Washington, D.C.

For Heather and Megan
—L.F.M.

Founded in 1888, the National Geographic Society is one of the largest nonprofit scientific and educational organizations in the world. It reaches more than 285 million people worldwide each month through its official journal, NATIONAL GEOGRAPHIC, and its four other magazines; the National Geographic Channel; television documentaries; radio programs; films; books; videos and DVDs; maps; and interactive media. National Geographic has funded more than 8,000 scientific research projects and supports an education program combating geographic illiteracy.

For more information, please call
1-800-NGS-LINE (647-5463) or write to the following address:
NATIONAL GEOGRAPHIC SOCIETY
1145 17th Street N.W., Washington, D.C. 20036-4688 U.S.A.

Visit us online at www.nationalgeographic.com/books
Librarians and teachers, visit us at www.ngchildrensbooks.org

For more information about special discounts for bulk purchases, please contact
National Geographic Books Special Sales: ngspecsales@ngs.org

For rights or permissions inquiries, please contact
National Geographic Books Subsidiary Rights: ngbookrights@ngs.org

Library of Congress Cataloging-in-Publication Data available from the publisher on request
Trade Paperback ISBN: 978-1-4263-0484-2
Reinforced Library Edition ISBN: 978-1-4263-0485-9

Printed in USA

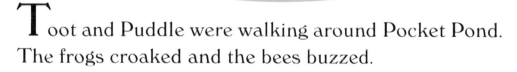

T oot and Puddle were walking around Pocket Pond.
The frogs croaked and the bees buzzed.

"Great music, isn't it?" said Puddle. But Toot didn't hear it.

"Listen. There's music all around you," Puddle
explained. He picked a grassy reed and started whistling.

"Wowie zowie!" said Toot. "I wish I could make music, too."

Suddenly, a taxi honked. "That's my ride to the airport."

Toot was ready to leave for his trip to Congo, Africa.

"I've read that the forests in Africa are full of music," said Puddle. "Maybe you could find some way to make music there."

"I'll sure try, Puds," said Toot.

"Have a great trip!" Puddle said with a wave.

As the plane landed in Congo, the flight attendant announced:
"We hope you've enjoyed your flight as in Congo we land,
Where the sounds of the forest become nature's own band.
While elephants stomp and gorillas parade,
Come see the marketplace, there's a lot to buy and trade."

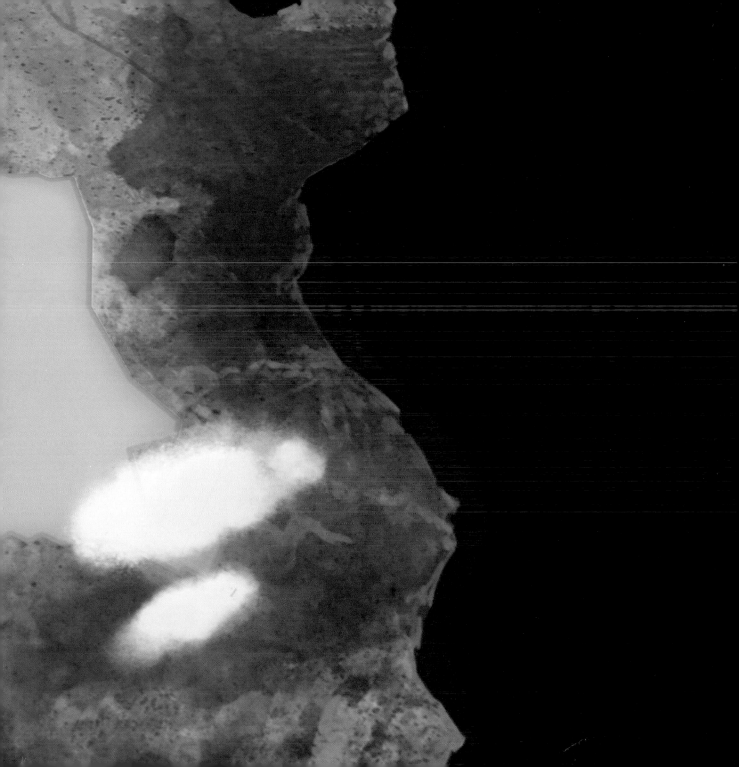

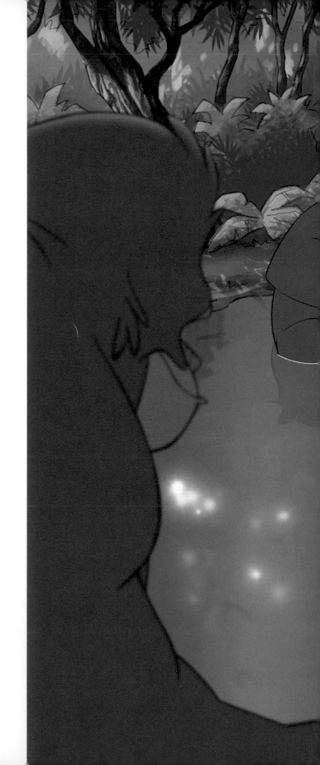

Once Toot arrived in Congo, he decided to explore the Ituri forest.

Toot admired the lush plants and birds he'd never seen before. When he came to a large river, Toot spied gorillas through the brush. They slapped the water with their palms. Plunk! Plop! Splash!

They're playing the river like a drum, thought Toot.

Toot heard a yelp in the trees above. With a whoosh, something came crashing down on him. When Toot opened his eyes, he saw a strange-looking pig.

"My name's Asani," the red river pig said. "I'm sorry for landing on you. My honey basket was too heavy."

When Asani discovered Toot was a visitor to the forest, he invited Toot back to his village for a feast.

That evening Asani explained that the feast was a way to thank the forest for its gifts. "If you take more than you need from the forest, it will not make music for you."

"The forest makes music?" Toot asked.

"Listen," replied Asani. "Can you hear the swirling wind, the bees buzzing near the hives, and the chattering monkeys? That is the music of the forest."

Toot *could* hear the music.

Then the animals brought out their instruments and began to play.

"Come, get with the beat, Toot!" said Asani, welcoming him to play his drum.

Toot didn't know how to play. He wasn't even sure how to start.

"Just let the sounds of the forest guide you," said Asani.

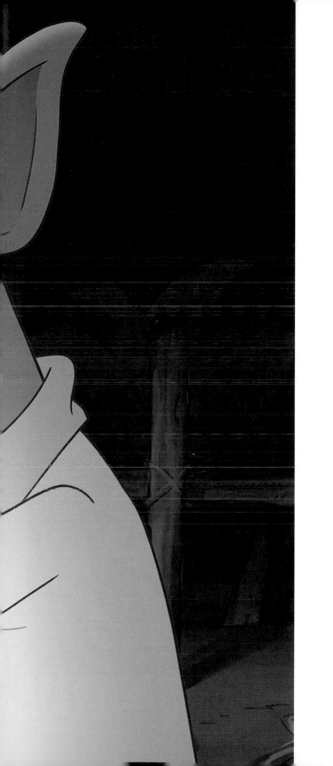

Toot listened carefully. He patted the drum once, then tried again. Toot began to feel the music and drummed a rhythmic beat.

Asani started singing. Now Toot was *really* drumming! They created a beautiful song.

When they were done, Toot took a picture with his new friends and their instruments to send to Puddle.

Several days later,
Puddle got the postcard in
the mail.
"It's from Toot!" Puddle said
to Tulip. "He's having fun in Congo.
Look at the drum he's playing."

Then Puddle heard a tap, tap, tap. It sort of sounded like a drum.

He found water dripping into a barrel outside. "This is almost the same shape as the drum on Toot's postcard!" he exclaimed. "I have an idea . . ."

Back in Congo, Toot was exploring. He found music everywhere he went!

He even climbed high up
in the treetops to help Asani
gather honey.

Toot wanted to take a drum back home to Puddle.

"You can get one from the market," Asani said. "You just need something to trade."

"Oh," said Toot, disappointed. "I don't have anything to offer."

"You can trade the basket of honey you've collected," suggested Asani.

"Great idea!" said Toot.

The next day, Toot found a stall selling drums at the market. "May I have that one please?" he asked.

"Is that honey I smell?" sniffed the drum seller.

Toot offered her a taste. "Yum. I'll accept your honey for the drum," she said. "Here you go."

"Now let's make music!" called Asani. "Toot, start us off."
Toot listened to the sounds around him. He heard the
wind rustling, birds calling, and monkeys chattering.
Toot began a steady beat on his drum. Then Asani joined
in. They each offered a different part in their beautiful song.

A few days later, it was time for Toot to leave Congo and return home to Pocket Hollow.

When Toot got out of the taxi, he heard drumming. *That sounds like a drum from Congo,* he thought. *But it can't be.*

He walked around to the back of the house to see where it was coming from.

"Welcome back, Toot!" said Puddle, beating a large barrel.

"That's amazing drumming!" Toot exclaimed.

"Thanks," Puddle beamed. "I made my drum look like the one in the picture you sent."

Toot held up the drum from Congo. "Let's play!"

And the two friends were off on a new adventure, making music together.